I've been in Little League for six years now. But to tell you the truth, I'm not what you'd call a real good athlete. Actually, I'm not even real fair. I'm more what you'd call real stinky.

Every year Alex Frankovitch—otherwise known as Skinnybones—receives the trophy for the Most Improved Player on his baseball team. That doesn't fool Alex, though. He knows that the only players who get that trophy are the ones "who stink to begin with." And with top-notch players like T.J. Stoner around to tease him, this season could end up being Alex's worst one yet.

Life looks hopeless when T.J. challenges Alex to a pitching contest (some contest!), and when Alex's new uniform (size small) is way too big, and especially when his losing team has to play T.J.'s winning one and a TV news crew decides to film that game! But Alex does have a hidden talent that could save the day, unless it ruins his whole life first. . . .

You'll laugh right along with Skinnybones in Barbara Park's new novel. It's the saddest, funniest baseball story of the season.

Skinnybones

by BARBARA PARK

ALFRED A. KNOPF • NEW YORK

To Steven and David
for all your inspiration

THIS IS A BORZOI BOOK
PUBLISHED BY ALFRED A. KNOPF, INC.

Copyright © 1982 by Barbara Park
Jacket painting copyright © 1982 by Rob Sauber
All rights reserved under International and Pan-American
Copyright Conventions. Published in the United States by
Alfred A. Knopf, Inc., New York, and simultaneously in
Canada by Random House of Canada Limited, Toronto.
Distributed by Random House, Inc., New York.

Library of Congress Cataloging in Publication Data
Park, Barbara.   Skinnybones.
Summary: Alex's active sense of humor helps him get
along with the school braggart, make the most of his
athletic talents, and simply get by in a hectic world.
I. Title   PZ7.P2197Sk   1982   [Fic]   81-20791
ISBN 0-394-84988-4   AACR2
ISBN 0-394-94988-9 (lib. bdg.)
Manufactured in the United States of America

20   19   18   17

SKINNYBONES

chapter one

MY CAT EATS KITTY FRITTERS BECAUSE . . .

I figure that if she *didn't* eat Kitty Fritters, she would probably be dead by now.

Kitty Fritters is the only cat food my mother will buy. She buys it because she says it's cheap. She says she doesn't care how it tastes, or what it's made out of. My mother is not the kind of person who believes that an animal is a member of the family. She is one of those people who thinks a cat is just a cat.

I have an aunt who thinks that her cat is a real person. Every time we go over there, she has her cat dressed up in this little sweater that says FOXY KITTY on the front.

This aunt of mine wouldn't be caught dead giving her cat Kitty Fritters. She says that Kitty Fritters taste like rubber. I'd hate to think that my aunt has actually tasted Kitty Fritters herself, but how else would she know? My mother says that my aunt is a very sick person.

Anyway, I think you should keep on making Kitty Fritters as long as there are people like my mother, who don't think cats mind eating rubber.

THE END

After I finished writing, I went to the closet and took the bag of Kitty Fritters off the bottom shelf. I turned to the back of the bag and read the rest of the directions. It said:

COMPLETE THIS SENTENCE:
MY CAT EATS KITTY FRITTERS BECAUSE ...
Then print your name and address on the entry
blank enclosed in this bag. Mail your entry to:

KITTY FRITTERS TV CONTEST
P. O. Box 2343
Philadelphia, Pennsylvania 19103

I dug down into the bag, trying to find the entry blank. I couldn't feel it anywhere. I tried again, reaching down into the other side of the bag. It wasn't there either. Finally I put the bag between my legs, and stuck both of my arms all the way down to the very bottom. I still couldn't find it!

Finally I got so frustrated, I dumped the entire ten-pound bag of cat food out onto the kitchen floor. I must have sifted through about a million little fritters before I finally found the entry blank. Carefully, I placed it on the kitchen counter and filled it out.

NAME: Alex Frankovitch
ADDRESS: 2567 Delaney Street
CITY: Phoenix   STATE: Arizona   ZIP: 85004

Just as I was finishing up, I heard the cat scratching at the door. I figured that she had probably smelled the disgusting odor of fritters all the way down the block.

"Go away!" I shouted. "You can't come in right now. I'm busy!"

I just *had* to get the cat food mess cleaned up before my mother got home.

"Alex Frankovitch! You open this door!" shouted my cat. My cat? Oh no! Suddenly, I realized that it had been my *mother* scratching at the door.

I hurried to let her in.

"Why were you scratching at the door?" I asked when I opened it. It was a very stupid question. She was carrying two large bags of groceries.

"I wasn't scratching," she answered as she hustled by me. "I banged on it with my foot!"

After putting the groceries on the counter, my mother glanced down at the millions of little fritters scattered all over the floor. All things considered, I think she took it very well.

"Been fixing yourself a little snack, Alex?" she asked, sounding slightly annoyed.

I figured that there were two different ways of handling my problem. First of all, I could try to get my mother to laugh about the whole thing. If *that* failed, I would have to move on to Plan Two: Blame It on the Cat.

"Snack? What snack?" I asked, trying to sound very serious. "I haven't been fixing a snack."

"I *mean* all these Kitty Fritters, Alex," said my mother, even more annoyed than before.

"Kitty Fritters?" I asked, looking all around. "What Kitty Fritters?"

This was where she was supposed to start laughing. But unfortunately, she didn't.

"I'm waiting for an explanation, Alex," she said, folding her arms. Whenever my mother folds her arms, she means business. Quickly, I moved on to Plan Two.

"Oh . . . *those* Kitty Fritters!" I said, pointing at the floor. "Well, you're probably not going to believe this, but while you were gone I was sitting in the den watching TV—"

"Now, *that* I believe," interrupted my mother. "It seems that all you've been doing lately is watching that stupid TV."

"Listen, Mother," I said, "do you want to hear what happened, or not?"

"Okay, Alex," she said, "you may continue."

"Well, anyway," I said, "there I was watching TV, when all of a sudden, I heard this loud crash come from the kitchen. I ran in here just in time to see the cat running out the back door. That's when I looked down and saw this giant mess of fritters."

My mother just stared at me for a minute. Then she said, "Are you *positive* that's what happened, Alex?"

I couldn't believe it. My mother was actually going to believe that stupid story. Wow! For the very first time, I was really going to get away with something. Usually I *never* get away with *anything*!

"Positive, Mom," I replied. "Honest, that's exactly what happened. The cat must have tried to get something to eat and knocked the bag over."

My mother walked over and put her hand on my shoulder. "In that case, Alex," she said, "could you please do me a big favor?"

"Aw, come on, Mom!" I said, trying to sound upset. "You're not going to make me clean this whole mess up, are you? That's really not fair. I just told you I didn't do it!"

"No, Alex, that's *not* what I wanted," she said with a very strange grin on her face. "What I want you to do is to go and get the cat out of the car. I just brought her home from the vet's. I took her to get her shots."

Now, most people think that when you get caught in a giant lie like that you're doomed. But not me. I've always said, "A good liar never gives up without a fight."

"Boy, that really makes me mad!" I shouted.

"What makes you mad, Alex?" asked my mother. "Being caught in a stupid, ridiculous lie like that?"

"Lie? What lie? What are you talking about, Mom? No," I said, "the thing that makes me mad is that one of Fluffy's little friends would come in here, make a big mess, and then try to run away

8

and blame it on poor little Fluffy! Boy, when I find out which neighborhood cat did this, he's *really* going to be sorry."

Then I hurried outside and got Fluffy from the car. As I walked back into the house, I kept talking to the cat so that my mother wouldn't have a chance to say anything.

"Fluffy, you're not going to believe this, but one of your little buddies almost got you in very big trouble! If you ask me, I think it was probably Fritzi, from down the street. I've always thought that Fritzi was the sneaky type—"

"Alex . . . Alex!" shouted my mother, interrupting me.

"Yes, Mom?"

"Give up," she said.

"Give up?" I asked. "What do you mean, give up?"

"I mean, you're making a fool out of yourself, Alex," she said.

I paused for a minute and looked up. "Does this mean that you don't believe me?"

"Let me put it this way, Alex," my mother replied. "If you were Pinocchio, right now we'd have enough firewood to last the winter."

Then she handed me a broom and started out of the room.

"Don't look so glum," she said as she left. "If it

will make you feel any better, that was the most creative fib you've told in weeks."

I thought about it.

It didn't make me feel better.

As soon as she was gone, I started sweeping the Kitty Fritters back into the bag. Meanwhile, Fluffy had begun to eat every single fritter in sight.

I just couldn't seem to get the darned things back into the bag fast enough. Fluffy was really packing them in. Getting shots must give cats quite an appetite.

It took about ten minutes before I was finished cleaning up the floor. By that time, I could tell that Fluffy was getting pretty full. But she never stopped eating . . . not until the last Kitty Fritter was in the bag.

As I put the bag back on the bottom shelf, my mother came in to inspect the floor. The cat ran to greet her. My mother stared at her for a minute.

"Why does Fluffy look so puffy?" she asked.

"I guess it must be all those Kitty Fritters she ate while I was trying to get them cleaned up," I explained.

"Oh, Alex!" my mother cried. "Those things will swell up in her stomach and make her very sick! She's not supposed to have too many!"

My mother looked worried.

I would have been worried too, but just then Fluffy walked over to where I was standing and threw up on my shoe. It was the most disgusting thing that ever happened to me.

My mother started laughing.

"This is not funny!" I shouted. But my mother couldn't seem to stop. If you ask me, I think she was acting pretty childish.

After a couple of minutes, she walked over and picked up the cat. "Honestly, Fluffy," she said, "if you don't like Alex's shoes, all you have to do is *say* so." Then she started laughing all over again.

I think I probably would have felt a lot worse, but my mother was laughing so hard that she forgot to punish me for lying to her. Getting her to laugh always works. I just wish I could have done it without having Fluffy throw up on me.

chapter two

The first time that I can remember making people laugh was in kindergarten. Every morning, the teacher would ask if anyone had anything special for Show and Tell.

At first I was pretty shy. I would just sit there quietly at my desk and keep my mouth shut. But there were lots of kids who didn't.

There was this one kid named Peter Donnelly who sat in front of me. Every single day, when the teacher asked if anyone had anything for Show and Tell, dumb old Peter Donnelly would raise his hand.

Sometimes he brought in hobbies. Peter had the stupidest hobbies in the whole world. One of his hobbies was collecting different-colored fuzz. Weird, right?

One day he brought his fuzz collection to school. He kept it in a shoe box. When he passed it around, I felt stupid just looking at it.

Then, all of a sudden, I got this funny idea. Just as I was about to pass the box to the next person, I pretended that I was going to sneeze.

"AH . . . AH . . . AHCHOO!"

I sneezed right smack in the middle of Peter's fuzz collection. Fuzz balls went flying everywhere. The whole class began to laugh at once.

Peter panicked. He rushed over to my desk and began gathering up his fuzz collection and putting it back in his box. The teacher told me to help him, but I was laughing too hard to get out of my chair. I had to admit, making people laugh was a lot more fun than sitting quietly in my seat. I decided I would have to do it more often.

From then on, I began to use Show and Tell to tell the class funny things that had happened to me. When I ran out of true things to tell, I started making them up.

One time I told the class that my father was a raisin. I don't know what made me say such a silly thing. But it sure sounded funny.

The teacher made me sit down. She said that

there was a big difference between Show and Tell and Show and Fib. Personally, I don't think teachers like it when their students are funnier than they are. I ought to know. So far I've been funnier than every teacher I've ever had. And not one of them has liked me. My goal in life is to try and find a teacher who appreciates my sense of humor.

Last year I had a teacher named Miss Henderson. So far, out of all the teachers I've ever had, Miss Henderson is the one who disliked me the most.

I'm not really sure why. In the fifth grade, I was the funniest I've ever been. You'd think a teacher would like it when a student tries to brighten up the day with a little joke or two.

On the very first day of school, I knew Miss Henderson wasn't going to like me. She made everyone stand up next to their desk and introduce themselves to the class. Boy, do I hate that! You were supposed to tell your name, where you were born, and something about your family. Allison Martin started.

She said, "My name is Allison Martin. I was born right here in Phoenix, and I have two brothers."

Whoopee for you, I thought to myself.

Then, Brenda Ferguson stood up. "My name

is Brenda Ferguson. I was born in California, and I have a baby sister."

And you're also very dumb, I thought.

This had to be the most boring thing I had ever listened to in my life. After about six kids had spoken, I just couldn't stand it anymore. I raised my hand.

"Yes," said Miss Henderson. "You there, in the yellow shirt."

I looked down at my shirt. Yup. It was yellow all right. I stood up.

"Miss Henderson," I said, "this is getting kind of boring. Couldn't we try to tell something a little more interesting about ourselves?"

Miss Henderson thought about it for a minute and then gave me a little smile.

"Okay, then," she said finally. "Why don't you start us off? Tell us who you are and something interesting about yourself."

Wow! I thought to myself. Maybe for once, I've got a teacher who is going to appreciate me.

"Okay," I said. "My name is Alex Frankovitch. I was born in Phoenix, and my mother is a land turtle."

Miss Henderson didn't laugh. Instead she gave me a dirty look and motioned for me to sit down.

By this time, the whole class was roaring, and

Miss Henderson had to beat on her desk with a ruler. For a minute there, I actually started feeling a little sorry for her. But it didn't last long. As soon as she got the class under control, she continued with the same boring stuff we had been doing before.

After about an hour, we were almost finished. That's when I first noticed T. J. Stoner. He was sitting all the way in the back of the room. He was the very last person to tell about himself.

When he got up, he said, "My name is T. J. Stoner. I just moved here from San Diego. I have an older brother who plays baseball for the Chicago Cubs." Then he sat back down and tried to look cool.

Boy, do I hate it when kids try to look cool. I knew right away I wasn't going to like T. J. Stoner.

"That's very interesting, T.J.," said Miss Henderson. You could tell she was really impressed. "Could you tell us a little bit more about yourself?"

"Well, okay." T.J. stood up again. "My brother's name is Matt Stoner, and he plays third base. This is his second year in the majors."

"Do you play baseball, too, T.J.?" asked Miss Henderson.

"Yes," said T.J., "I'm a pitcher. Last year my team won the state championship in California. I was voted the Most Valuable Player."

"My goodness!" screeched Miss Henderson. "It really sounds as though you'll be playing for the Cubs someday yourself!"

Yuck! This whole conversation was making me sick! I raised my hand and began waving it all over the place. I could tell that Miss Henderson didn't want to call on me, but I was pretty hard to ignore.

"Yes?" she said, sounding disgusted.

I stood up. "Miss Henderson," I began, "I just thought that the class might like to know that I play baseball, too." She just kept staring at me, with her hands on her hips. I continued. "Last season, I played center field. At the end of the year, I was voted the Player with the Slowest Mother."

The whole class roared. Brenda Ferguson laughed so hard she almost fell off her chair. But two people didn't laugh at all. One was Miss Henderson. The other was T. J. Stoner.

I decided to sit down and keep my mouth shut for a while. The good thing about me is that I usually know when to quit. I may be funny, but I'm not stupid.

chapter three

Sometimes I think it would be fun to be a school principal . . . especially in the summer. A school principal spends his summers making up lists of all the kids in the school who hate each other. Then he makes sure he puts them together in the same class.

He really must have had a good laugh when he put T.J. and me in the same room again this year. Ever since I got sent to the principal for wearing wax lips to music class, he hasn't seemed to like me much.

When I first discovered the bad news about T.J., I hurried to tell my mother. I was hoping that maybe she could call the school and have me switched to a different classroom or something.

But no such luck. All my mother did was tell me that I should try to ignore him. She's always giving me great advice like that. Then she hands me my lunch, shoves me out the door, and her problems are over for the day. Mine are just beginning.

Last year, T. J. Stoner grew to be the biggest kid in the whole fifth grade. When I began to notice how big he was getting, I decided it might not be a bad idea to try to make friends with him. But unfortunately, T.J. didn't seem too interested. If I remember correctly, his exact words were, "Get lost, creep-head."

"Does that mean no?" I asked.

T.J. grabbed me by the shoulders and looked me straight in the eye. Then he said, "It means I hate your guts, Alex!"

"Aw come on, T.J.," I said, smiling. "Can't our guts be friends?"

T.J. didn't think that was quite as funny as I did. I could tell by the way he pushed me down and sat on my head. "Stop being such a jerk, you skinny bag of bones. You're beginning to get on my nerves." He gave me another shove and left. It's too bad my mother wasn't there. Maybe she could have told me how to ignore someone's knee when it's shoved in your mouth.

I think the worst thing about being in the same room with T.J. is having him in my gym class. I hate to admit it, but he's really a great athlete. For a kid, T. J. Stoner is the best baseball player that I've ever seen.

There's only one sport that I'm better at than T.J.—square dancing. I figure I can count square dancing as a sport because we do it in gym. You ought to see me. I can promenade my partner better than any other kid in the whole school.

One time I asked the gym teacher, Mr. McGuinsky, if he ever thought about starting a school square dancing team. I told him that if he did, I would like to volunteer to be the team captain.

He must have thought I was making a joke. He told me to sit my tail down and shut up. Gym teachers like to say "tail" a lot.

I do play other sports besides square dancing. Take Little League for instance. I've been in Little League for six years now. But to tell you the truth, I'm not what you'd call a real good athlete. Actually, I'm not even real fair. I'm more what you'd call real stinky.

I've got proof, too. Every single year that I've

played Little League, I've received the trophy for the Most Improved Player.

You may think that means I'm pretty good. That's what *I* used to think, too. But, over the past six years, I've noticed that none of the really good players ever gets the Most Improved Player award. And I finally figured out why. It's because the good players are already so good that they can't improve much. Let's face it, the only players on a team who can improve are the players who stink to begin with.

Last year, at the end of baseball season, I tried to explain how I felt to my father. We were sitting together at the Little League awards ceremony. The announcer began calling the names of all the players who were going to be receiving trophies.

I started to get very nervous.

"Just relax, Alex," said my father. "It won't be the end of the world if you don't win Most Improved again this year."

He just didn't understand at all.

"That's just it, Dad," I said, trying to explain. "I don't *want* to get Most Improved again. I don't mean to be a poor sport or anything, but if they call my name, why don't we just pretend we're not here. What do you say, Dad?"

I could tell by his face that my father was shocked. "Pretend we're not here!" he said loudly. "What kind of sportsmanship do you call that?"

"Shhh . . . Dad . . . not so loud," I said, trying to quiet him down. "It's just too embarrassing to get *another* Improved award, that's all. I just don't want it."

"I can't believe you!" my father exclaimed. "How ungrateful can you get, Alex? Do you know how many kids here would *love* to get that award tonight?"

"I know, Dad," I answered, "but that's only because most of them haven't figured out what the Most Improved trophy really means. They don't understand that getting that award means that you were *really* a stink-o player at the beginning of the season. Big deal. I'm supposed to be happy because I've gone from being stink-o to just smelly."

About that time, I heard my name being called over the microphone.

"Alex Frankovitch. Most Improved Player award for team number seven, Preston's Pest Control!"

When I heard it, I slid way down in my seat so that no one could see me. I could tell that my father was *very* annoyed with the way I was acting. He kept trying to grab my arm and make me stand up. Instead, I doubled over even further, and put my head between my knees.

The announcer called my name again. "Alex Frankovitch? Is Alex here?" he bellowed.

My father jumped up from his seat and pointed at me. At least that's what I *think* he did. I couldn't be sure. I was too busy trying to wad myself up into a little ball.

"Here he is, right here," screamed my dad. "Alex Frankovitch is right here!"

I guess everyone thought I was just being shy. The next thing I knew, the announcer shouted, "Let's give Alex a little applause to get him down here!"

Everyone started clapping. Then a few of the kids who knew me started shouting, "WE WANT ALEX . . . WE WANT ALEX!"

Finally, I had no choice. I stood up and started making my way down the bleachers. By the time I reached the fifth row, I had decided that I would never speak to my father again.

When I got to the bottom, I spotted T. J. Stoner. He was there getting another Most Valuable Player trophy. He kept pointing at me and laughing . . . pointing and laughing. . . .

I just couldn't let him get away with making fun of me. I decided that the only thing I could do was to pretend that I was really enjoying myself.

I walked to the middle of the gym floor, turned around, and started taking bows and throwing kisses. Then I walked over to the table to pick up my trophy.

The announcer handed me the microphone as I received my award. I was supposed to say thank you. But instead, I took the microphone, held it up to my mouth and burped.

The whole crowd started laughing at once. At least that's the way it sounded. Actually, I think the only people laughing were the kids. Usually, grownups don't think burping is quite as funny as kids do.

After that I decided to walk home. I knew I was in trouble, so I went straight to my room and waited for my father.

While I was waiting, I made a sign and hung it on the outside of my door. The sign said:

THIS ROOM BELONGS TO ALEX FRANKOVITCH,
THE ONLY BOY IN THE WHOLE WORLD
WHO HAS GONE FROM STINK-O TO SMELLY
SIX YEARS IN A ROW.

When my father saw the sign, he didn't even bother coming into my room to yell at me. I guess he figured I already felt bad enough.

He was right.

chapter four

For me, the worst part about belonging to Little League is the uniforms. Every year, the same thing happens. This year, at my second practice, it happened again.

The coach makes everyone line up to tell him what size shirt and pants they needed. He calls out a name and we shout out our size. We have three choices: small, medium, or large.

I checked out the other kids on my team. There were twelve of us all together. I figured that out of our whole team there were five larges, six mediums, and one teeny-tiny . . . me.

Every single year I am the smallest kid on the team. For a long time, I actually thought that I was a midget.

I remember when I was in first grade our teacher asked us to cut out magazine pictures of what we thought we would look like when we grew up. Most of the guys in my class brought in pictures of baseball or football players. A couple of others brought in pictures of policemen.

I brought in a picture of a Munchkin.

I got it out of *TV Guide*. Munchkins are the short little guys that keep running all over the place in the movie, *The Wizard of Oz*.

I think my teacher was surprised when she saw my picture. She called me up to her desk.

"Alex, what is this a picture of?" she asked.

"It's a Munchkin," I answered.

"That's what I was afraid of," she said.

"Oh, you don't have to be afraid of Munchkins, Mrs. Hurley," I said. "They're too short to hurt anyone."

"I *know* that they're short, Alex," she replied. "What I don't understand is why you want to be one when you grow up."

"I don't," I answered. "I want to be a baseball player."

"Then why did you bring in this picture?" asked Mrs. Hurley.

"Because *that's* what I'm going to look like," I explained. "You said to bring in a picture of what we were going to *look* like, didn't you?"

I guess Mrs. Hurley must have been worried about me. When I got home from school that day, she had already called my mother. As soon as I walked in the door, Mom sat me down and had a nice long talk with me about midgets.

"Alex," said my mother, "I know that you think you're too short. But that's only because you haven't started to grow as much as some of the other kids. Everyone grows at *different* speeds. But, believe me, you are going to grow! You are *not* going to be a Munchkin."

Then she took me by the hand and led me to the kitchen. She stood me up against the wall near the corner and told me not to move.

For a minute I thought she was going to try to shoot an apple off my head or something. Instead, she got a pencil and made a mark on the wall behind me. When I moved away, she wrote the date right next to it.

"Now," she said, "just to prove to you how much you're growing, we will measure you every six months. You won't believe it until you see it."

Well, all I can say is six months is a long time to wait . . . especially when you're waiting to find out whether or not you're a midget.

When the day finally came to measure me again, I was pretty nervous about it.

My mother stood me up against the wall in the same spot where I had been measured before. Then she carefully made another pencil mark. When I turned to look at it, I was *very* relieved. I had grown almost half an inch.

"Now do you believe me?" asked my mother. "Does this prove to you that you're not going to be a Munchkin?"

"Yeah, I guess so," I answered. "Now, if I could only figure out a way to put on some weight."

My mother threw her hands in the air. "I give up!" she shouted. "Honestly, Alex, if it's not one problem, it's another!" Then she just shook her head and left the room.

Sometimes my mother doesn't understand me at all. Being small is not an easy thing to be. Especially when you have to shout it out in front of your whole entire baseball team.

"Alex Frankovitch?" yelled my coach, "Small, medium, or large?"

I just couldn't bring myself to say 'small.' In fact, I guess you could say I panicked.

"Large!" I shouted.

Everyone on the team turned around to look at me. A couple of them laughed.

The coach walked over to me.

"Did you say 'large,' Alex?" he asked.

"Yes sir," I answered. "Large."

"Are you *sure* that large is the size you take, Alex?" he asked.

"Oh, no sir," I answered. "I usually don't take a large."

The coach looked relieved. "Well, what size do you usually take?"

"Extra large," I answered.

He just looked at me for a minute and then scribbled something down on his paper. As he walked away he mumbled something to himself that sounded a lot like "bubble-head." But I really didn't care what he thought. At least I didn't have to shout out 'small' in front of the whole team.

I figured that the day the uniforms came would be the best day of my entire life. I even had a dream about it.

In my dream, the coach had all the uniforms arranged in two piles . . . small and large.

Then he stood up and began calling out our names and sizes. When your name and size were called, you were supposed to go to the correct pile and select your uniform.

"Alex Frankovitch . . . large!" he shouted, loud enough for everyone to hear.

Slowly, I stood up and walked over to the large pile to choose my pants and shirt. When I got there, I realized that my uniform was the only one in the large pile. Everyone else on my team was a small. As I reached down to pick up my large shirt, everyone started to clap.

It was the best dream I ever had.

Finally, after waiting for three whole weeks for my dream to come true, the team uniforms came in. I was so excited I could hardly stand it.

When I got to practice that day, I noticed that the coach had arranged the uniforms in three piles. My heart started pounding wildly. It was almost like my dream. I felt like I had seen into the future or something.

Everyone lined up and the coach told us to go to the correct pile and pick out a uniform. This wasn't quite as good as if he had called out my name and size, but I really didn't mind. All I really cared about was having everyone see me at the large pile.

As soon as it was my turn, I rushed over and grabbed a large shirt and a pair of pants. I hung around the pile for a few seconds so everyone could see me, and then I took my uniform and stood back so the other kids could get theirs. When all the piles were gone, the coach told us to check our uniforms to make sure we had chosen the right size.

All of a sudden, I heard a few of the guys start to laugh. I turned around and saw Randy Tubbs trying to pull his new shirt over his head. It was stuck on his ears. Randy Tubbs is the biggest kid on our team. His head probably weighs as much as my entire body.

"Hey, Coach," he shouted, "I think I've got a little problem here!"

The coach walked over and helped Randy get the shirt off his head. Then he looked inside to see what size it was.

"This is a small, Randy," he said. "You ordered a large."

"Yeah," said Randy, "but this was the only uniform left when I got there."

The coach started looking all around. All of a sudden, I got this real sick feeling in my stomach. I tried to sneak off the practice field, but as I was walking away, he spotted me.

"Hold it, Alex," said the coach. "Bring your uniform over here for a minute, would you?"

As I handed the coach my shirt and pants, I checked the tag. "See, Coach? It's a large, just like you ordered for me," I said.

"Alex, I ordered you a small," he said. Then

he gave my uniform to Randy and handed me the small.

Boy, did that ever make me mad. What gave him the right to steal my uniform like that?

Randy held up his new shirt. "Now *that's* better!" he said, smiling.

When I got home I tried on my uniform. I sure didn't have any trouble getting it over my head. Good old Randy had really stretched the neck out of shape. It hung down to my stomach!

My mother told me not to worry about it. She said the shirt would probably shrink a little when it was washed. I didn't tell her, but I wished the pants would shrink too. They were way too big.

chapter five

T. J. Stoner brags about his baseball team more than any kid I've ever known in my whole life. So what if his team hasn't lost a game all year? It doesn't mean they won just because of T.J. Everyone knows that one kid can't make the difference between a winning team and a losing team. After all, every team *I've* ever been on has come in last place. And I don't care what anyone says, all those teams didn't lose just because of me.

This year I happen to know that I am not the worst player on my team. The worst player on my team is Ryan Brady. Ryan doesn't help us out at all. The very first game of the season, Ryan broke his arm. Now all he does is sit on the bench. I'm sure I help the team out a lot more than Ryan.

I play center field. A lot of kids think that if you play in the outfield, it means you stink. My father says that's ridiculous. He says that outfielders are just as important as infielders. He told me that when he was a boy, he played in the outfield just like me. But that doesn't really make me feel much better. I've seen my father play baseball. He stinks.

My mother says that when people like T. J. Stoner brag, it's just because they're trying to get attention. And, as usual, she says to ignore them. But, for some reason, whenever I hear T.J. start to brag about his baseball team, I just can't seem to keep my mouth shut.

One day, a couple of weeks ago, I heard him talking to a bunch of kids out on the playground.

"My coach told me that for a kid, I was the best pitcher he had ever seen in his life," he said.

When I heard *that*, I did a very dumb thing. I called over to my friend Brian Dunlop. "Hey, Brian," I shouted, "I forgot to tell you. Last night, at baseball practice, my coach let me pitch. And boy, was he impressed! He said that I threw the fastest ball he had ever seen!"

I *know* it was a ridiculous thing to say, but

Brian sure wasn't much help. When he heard what I was saying, he fell on the ground and started laughing. I guess I really couldn't blame him, though. Brian has seen me throw.

Pretty soon, T.J. came strolling over. He bent over to talk to Brian. "Did I hear Skinnybones say that he can throw a fast ball?"

Brian couldn't stop laughing long enough to answer, so he just nodded his head.

T.J. stood up and walked over to where I was standing. "Hey, Frankovitch," he said, "I'll make you a little deal."

"Gee, I'm sorry, T.J.," I answered, shaking my head. "If you're going to try and get me to come pitch for your team, you're too late. The Yankees already called me this morning."

Brian let out another wild scream of laughter. T.J. joined him. I guess the idea of me pitching was even funnier than I thought.

One time I tried pitching with my dad. But it really didn't work out very well. Most of the balls I threw didn't even make it to the plate. Eight of them bounced in the dirt. The only ball that made it over the plate beaned him on the head.

"What kind of a stupid pitch was that?" shouted my father as he rubbed his head.

"I call it my old bean ball!" I shouted back.

I guess he wasn't in the mood for jokes that day. We packed up our stuff and went home.

Anyway, after T.J. finally stopped laughing about my big offer from the Yankees, he started bugging me again.

"Come on, Alex," he begged, "just listen to my deal. What have you got to lose?"

By this time a bunch of kids had started to gather around us. I think most of them had come over to see what was wrong with Brian.

"Okay, T.J.," I said, "tell your deal. But make it snappy. It's almost time for Brian to massage my pitching arm."

"Okay," said T.J. "This is it. Since we're both such good pitchers, let's hold a contest after school to see who's the best. We'll even get a couple of kids to be the official umpires. What do you say, Frankovitch, is it a deal or not?"

Geez, what a mess I was in! If I said no, everyone would think I was chicken. But, if I said yes, everyone would be able to see how badly I pitched. I just had to get out of it!

I thought about it for a couple of minutes before I answered. "Gee, I'd really *love* to, T.J.," I answered finally. "But my coach told me not to tire my arm out by being in any stupid pitching contests. Thanks anyway."

I started to walk away but T.J. grabbed me by the shoulders. "You get one of your friends, Frankovitch, and I'll get one of mine. They'll be the umps. I'll meet you at the Little League field after school. If you're not there, we'll all know it's just because you're chicken."

As he turned to walk away, he stopped and looked back at me. "Be there, creep-head!" he shouted.

After he was gone, I looked down at Brian. He was still on the ground.

"Hey, Brian," I said, "how would you like to be an umpire this afternoon?"

Brian nodded his head. I think his sides were still hurting from all that laughing.

I reached my hand out to help him up. Together, we started back to class.

"Geez, Brian," I said, "if you think this is funny, wait until you see me pitch."

Then both of us started laughing. I figured I'd better laugh now while I had the chance.

chapter six

I was hoping the afternoon would drag on and on, but before I knew it the three o'clock bell rang. My teacher, Mrs. Grayson, dismissed the class.

I didn't want to go.

"Listen, Mrs. Grayson," I said, as she was getting ready to leave. "How would you like some help cleaning the boards and erasers this afternoon?"

"No thanks, Alex," she replied, "I've got a meeting to go to."

"Mrs. Grayson!" I said, trying to sound shocked, "I'm surprised at you! Do you mean to tell me that you are actually going to leave the room looking like a pig pen?"

"Please, Alex," she replied, "no jokes, okay? I'm really in a hurry." She held the door open for me to leave.

"Exactly what kind of meeting are you going to, Mrs. Grayson?" I asked.

"It's just a teachers' meeting, Alex, that's all. But I don't want to be late, so let's go, huh?"

"Listen, Mrs. Grayson," I continued. "How would you like it if I came along with you? That way, if the meeting got real boring, we could play tic-tac-toe, or something."

Mrs. Grayson stopped rushing me out the door. "Alex, is there some *reason* that you don't want to leave school today?" she asked. "Are you in some sort of trouble?"

"Trouble? Me?" I answered. "Oh no, Mrs. Grayson. Not me! I was just trying to make your meeting a little more fun, that's all."

"Well, thanks anyway, Alex," she said, "but I think I'll be able to stay awake today."

"Okay, have it your own way," I said, "but don't say I didn't try to help. I guess I'll just be heading on home now, Mrs. Grayson. That is, unless you'd like me to stick around until after your meeting's over to help you erase the boards. . . ."

I think Mrs. Grayson was getting a little

annoyed with me. "Go home, Alex!" she shouted.

So I did. I went home and got my ball and glove. Then I called Brian and told him to meet me at the Little League field.

By the time I got there, everyone else was already waiting for the contest to begin. And, when I say everyone, I mean *everyone*. There must have been about a million kids standing around waiting for me to make a big fool out of myself.

"Hey, Frankovitch!" shouted T.J., when he saw me coming. "For a minute there, I didn't think you were going to show up. What took you so long? Were you home plucking your feathers?"

I think this was his way of calling me a chicken again.

"A turkey like you probably knows a lot about feathers, T.J.!" I shouted back.

A few of the kids standing around started to laugh. T.J. wasn't one of them. He walked over to me.

"This is what we're going to do, Frankovitch," he began, seriously. "I brought along a catcher. He'll be catching for both of us."

I looked over at the kid in the catcher's mask. It was Hank Grover, one of T.J.'s best friends.

41

"Not fair! Not fair!" I protested. "I should have gotten to bring my own catcher, too!"

"What difference does it make who catches?" he asked. "The catcher isn't going to call balls or strikes. The umpires are going to do that. And besides, Alex," he added, "none of your jerky little friends knows how to catch."

Boy, did that ever make me mad! Insulting my friends like that! I probably should have punched him right in the mouth. Except for one tiny little problem. He was right. None of my jerky little friends *can* catch.

"Okay," T.J. continued, "we're each going to pitch ten balls. Your umpire and my umpire will stand together behind home plate. Then, as each ball is thrown, they will decide whether it's a strike or a ball. And to make it fair, the umpires *have* to agree on every call. If they can't agree, the pitcher takes the whole thing over again. Does that seem fair to you, Frankovitch?"

"Yeah, I guess so," I said. By this time I was getting nervous. All I *really* wanted to do was go home.

T.J. took a dime out of his pocket. "We'll flip to see who gets to pitch first," he said.

"Gee, I'm really sorry, T.J.," I said. "But I guess we won't be able to have this contest after all. I never learned how to flip. Maybe we could just somersault to see who goes first."

"Very funny. Now, heads or tails?" he yelled as he threw the coin in the air.

"Tummies," I hollered, trying to look very serious.

"Listen, Alex!" he yelled. "Knock off the funny stuff. Now . . . I'm going to toss this up one more time—heads or tails?" he shouted again.

I called tails.

It was heads. A bad sign.

"Okay," said T.J., "I won the toss, so I'll go first."

He took his ball and glove to the pitcher's mound. T.J.'s umpire, Eddie Fowler, and my umpire, Brian, took their places behind home plate. I hated to admit it, but having two umpires really did seem very fair. The trouble was, it seemed a little too fair. Before T.J. started pitching, I decided to have a little talk with Brian. I called him over.

"Listen, Brian," I said, "just because T. J. Stoner happens to be the very best pitcher that we've ever seen, doesn't mean that he's *perfect*. So, whatever you do, don't be afraid to call one of his pitches a ball if you really think it's a ball. And I don't want you to think that I would ever try to get you to cheat or anything, but keep in mind that I will be glad to pay you a dime for every ball you call—"

T.J. saw me talking to Brian and shouted, "Hey, Alex, don't bother trying to get Brian to cheat for you. I told him before you got here that if I caught him cheating, I'd break his face."

Brian looked at me and smiled. "Sorry, Alex," he said, "but I think I'd rather keep my face than make a couple of lousy dimes."

I was doomed.

T.J. was all set. "I'm ready!" he shouted.

"Ready?" I yelled back. "Aren't we even going to get a couple of practice pitches or anything?"

"You can practice if you *need* to, Frankovitch," he hollered, "but I don't really want any."

T.J. went into his windup. Some kids look dumb when they're winding up. But T.J. looked just like Steve Carlton.

Then he threw. The ball hit the catcher's mitt at about sixty miles an hour. But even worse, it hit his glove *exactly* in the center.

"Strike one!" shouted both umpires together.

T.J. didn't even blink an eye. He just got ready to throw the next pitch.

"Strike two!" shouted the umpires as the

second pitch crossed the middle of the plate.

This time, T.J. looked over in my direction and smiled. I leaned down and pretended I was tying my shoe so I wouldn't have to look at him.

"What's the matter, Alex?" he shouted. "Is the ball flying by so fast that it's untying your shoes?"

Then he laughed and got ready for his third pitch. As usual, it was perfect. The guy was really beginning to make me sick.

Every single pitch he threw came whizzing over the plate so fast you could hardly even see it. The catcher never even had to move a muscle. The ball hit the center of his mitt ten times straight! It was really disgusting.

"Okay, Skinnybones," he yelled after he'd thrown his last pitch, "it's your turn."

As T.J. sat down on the sidelines, Brian walked over and patted me on the back.

"Some friend you turned out to be, Brian," I said angrily. "What's the matter, did you forget how to say the word 'ball'?"

"Oh, get off it, Alex," he answered. "All his pitches were perfect. You really didn't expect me to cheat, did you?"

"Great, Brian," I said. "I'll remember how you feel about cheating the next time you need help on a math test."

Then I grabbed my glove and slowly walked out to the pitcher's mound. I was hoping that maybe, if I walked slowly enough, it would be dark by the time I got there and everyone would have to go home to dinner. But unfortunately, when I got to the mound the sun was still shining. There was no getting out of it now. I took a deep breath and turned around.

Oh no! It was a lot farther to home plate than I remembered. I began to panic. I can't throw all the way from here! I thought to myself. I'm so far away, the two umpires look like midgets!

Just then the two umpires stood up. Whew! That was a close one. They must have sat down when they saw how long it was taking me to get out to the mound.

The umpires lined up behind home plate and the catcher got set.

"Are you ready yet, Skinnybones?" yelled T.J. "Or do you want to practice first?"

Aha! A perfect opportunity to stall for time! Slowly, I walked off the mound and headed for T.J. on the sidelines. As soon as I got there he stood up. I stood on tiptoe and tried to look him in the eye.

"For your information, T.J.," I said, trying to act tough, "there is nothing skinny about my bones. So I would appreciate it if you would stop calling me that stupid name."

T.J. grabbed hold of my arm and held it up next to his.

"If your bones aren't skinny," he said, "then why is my arm so much bigger than yours?"

"You've got fat skin," I said simply.

T.J.'s eyes started getting real squinty. That meant he was about to hit me, so I hurried back out to the mound before he had a chance.

I stood there for a few minutes trying to figure out how to begin my windup. But pretty soon some of the kids started shouting at me to hurry up. So finally I was forced to begin.

I pulled my glove back toward my chest and stared at the catcher's mitt. Then I raised my left leg high in the air and hopped on my right foot.

Both of the umpires started to giggle. The catcher fell right over in the dirt laughing. They didn't even give me a chance to throw.

"Time out!" I yelled. "No fair! Interference on the umpires and the catcher!"

For once in his life, T.J. seemed to agree with me. He went over and tried to get the three of them to calm down. It took a few minutes, but finally they got themselves under control.

Once again, I went into my windup. I pulled

my glove back to my chest, raised my left leg high into the air, hopped on my right foot, and let the ball go.

I watched carefully as it rolled all the way to the plate. Wow! I thought to myself. What a pitch! It was a little low, of course, but at least I had it going in the right direction.

"Ball one!" shouted both umpires together.

"Well, I guess that's it, T.J.," I called as I walked off the mound. "I lost. One little mistake on my first pitch and it's all over. There's no way I can win, or even tie your pitching record when I've already got a ball. It's really a shame, too. That's probably the only bad pitch I'd have thrown all day."

"Not so fast, Frankovitch!" screamed T.J. running after me. He caught up to me and grabbed me by the collar. "You have nine more balls to throw, hot shot. We had a deal. So get back to that mound and we'll just see how good you are."

I knew there was no sense trying to argue with him. So slowly I turned around and headed back. Maybe there's still hope, I thought. If only I could throw a couple of good solid strikes, just one or two, at least I wouldn't end up looking like such an idiot.

I took a deep breath and got ready to throw my second pitch. My windup was the same, but something terrible happened when I started to throw. As I took the ball behind my head, it slipped out of my hand and landed in the dirt three feet behind me.

By this time I had really had it. All I wanted to do was get the whole thing over with quickly so I could go home and die. Brian had fallen in the dirt laughing. His mouth formed the words "Ball two," but nothing came out. I wound up and threw my third pitch as hard as I could.

T.J. was still watching from the sidelines. Unfortunately, my aim was a little bit off and the ball hit him in the arm.

"Strike one!" I shouted myself.

T.J. came running over holding his arm. "What do you mean, strike one?" he demanded, grabbing my shirt.

"Well, it struck you, didn't it?" I said, giggling.

"Let's see how you like being struck, Skinny-bones," he yelled, punching my arm as hard as he could.

Then he punched me again.

"Just remember what this feels like the next time you want to hit me with a ball," he growled. Somehow I got the feeling the contest was over.

My arm was a goner. It just hung limp at my side like it had croaked or something. I checked it out to see if it was bleeding, but no such luck. I hate that. When something hurts as bad as my arm did, the least it could do is bleed a little.

As T.J. walked away a lot of kids started running after him. Most of them were patting him on the arm and telling him what a great pitcher he was.

It's a good thing I didn't win. If anyone had patted me on my arm, I'm sure it would have fallen right off into the dirt.

I waited around a few minutes to walk home with Brian, but he must have left without me. At first I was mad about it, but in a way I understood. I guess he was just too embarrassed to walk home with a loser. I knew exactly how he felt. I didn't want to walk home with me, either.

chapter seven

Sometimes I wonder why I even bother to play baseball at all. I hate the uniforms, I can't throw, and I don't like playing center field. Lately I've been giving this a lot of thought, and there's only one thing I can come up with. . . .

I play for the caps.

Baseball caps are probably the greatest invention of all time. No matter what you look like, as soon as you put on a baseball cap you look just like Steve Garvey. Even my cat looks like Steve Garvey with my cap on.

Once I did an experiment with my grandmother just to prove it. My grandmother's about eighty years old, but she doesn't look it. She doesn't need a cane and she only wears glasses when she reads.

One of the things I like best about my grandmother is her blue hair. It's just about the coolest hair I've ever seen. I'm not sure that she really knows it's blue. I think she might be a little bit color-blind. One time at dinner she told my mother that she puts a "steel gray" rinse on it. I started to tell her that it looked more like "steel blue," but my mother stuck a roll in my mouth.

Anyway, after we finished eating that night, I ran up to my room and grabbed my baseball cap. Then I snuck up behind my grandmother and put it on her head. Just as I thought! Another Steve Garvey!

My grandmother wasn't a very good sport about it. She pulled my cap off her head and dropped it on the floor. Boy, I had really messed up her blue hair! In fact it was so messy that, right at the top of her head, I noticed a little bald spot. I offered to let her put my cap back on but she ignored me. I really felt sorry for her. She must have gone to the same barber I go to. My barber, Mr. Peoples, has given me more bald spots than I can even count.

I'll never forget the time he made my head look like a grapefruit. As soon as I walked in his shop that day, I knew I was in trouble. I always think it's a good idea to find out what kind of mood Mr. Peoples is in before I sit down in his chair. Sometimes when barbers aren't feeling very happy, they like to give kids funny haircuts to cheer themselves up.

"Hi, Mr. Peoples," I said with a smile. "How are you feeling today?"

Mr. Peoples looked at me and frowned. "I'll tell you how I'm feeling," he growled. "I'm hot, tired, and hungry. Any more questions?"

"Ah . . . no, Mr. Peoples, no more questions," I said as I began backing out of his shop. "Gee, I think I hear my mother calling. Maybe I'd better come back tomorrow."

"Knock it off, Alex, and sit down," he ordered, giving me a real disgusted look. Mr. Peoples has known me since I was two, so he thinks he can talk to me like that.

"Are you positive you want me to sit down?" I asked. "I mean, if you're not in a good mood I'd be happy to leave you alone for a little while."

"Sit!" he said gruffly, pointing to the chair.

Slowly I climbed into the big red seat. "Well, okay," I agreed. "But I really don't need a big haircut. I'd just like you to take a little bit off the sides. Okay?"

Mr. Peoples didn't hear a word I said. He was too busy plugging in his electric clippers.

"Wait a minute, Mr. Peoples!" I said quickly. "Do you really think you need the clippers today? I just want a little trim, remember?"

"Who's the barber here, Alex, you or me?" he asked sharply.

That's when I decided to be quiet. If there was one thing I didn't want to do, it was make the guy any madder than he already was.

Mr. Peoples started clipping. No wait . . . clipping is the wrong word. Mr. Peoples started scalping.

"You would have made a great Indian, Mr. Peoples," I said. But the clippers were so loud, he didn't hear me.

He whizzed those loud buzzing clippers all around the back of my head and headed up toward my ears.

All of a sudden, I heard him say, "Whoopsie!"

"Whoopsie?" I asked, nervously. "Did you just say 'whoopsie,' Mr. Peoples?"

I looked in the mirror. Right over my left ear, I saw the 'whoopsie.' It was a big round bald spot.

"This may be just a little bit shorter than you wanted it, Alex," said Mr. Peoples. "But at least it will be nice and cool for the summer."

"Nice and cool?" I asked angrily. "How do you figure that? If there are anymore 'whoopsies' I'll have to spend the whole summer wearing a big brown bag over my head. Have you ever spent the summer in a paper bag, Mr. Peoples?"

"Look on the bright side, Alex," he replied. "Think how easy it will be to take care of. Instead of combing through a lot of hair, all you'll have to do is polish your head a little." Then he laughed.

I couldn't stand to look in the mirror anymore so I closed my eyes and waited until he was finished. After circling my head with the clippers about twenty more times, he finally shut them off.

Slowly I opened my eyes and looked into the mirror. I couldn't believe it! I've seen more hair on an egg! I turned my head and looked at it from every angle hoping to find hair. But it was all gone.

"How do you like it?" asked Mr. Peoples, handing me a mirror.

"How do I like what?" I growled.

"Your hair, of course," he answered.

I gazed down at the floor. "I liked it a lot better when it was on my head," I replied as Mr. Peoples got the broom and started to sweep my hair into the dustpan.

55

He laughed. "I guess that means you think it's a little too short, huh?"

"No, Mr. Peoples," I answered. "If it was too short, at least some of it would still be growing out my head. I'd say it's too gone."

He laughed again. "That will be five dollars," he said, holding out his hand.

I slapped the money down and ran home as fast as I could. My mother met me at the door.

"Look what that butcher did to me!" I yelled, pointing to my head.

My mother stared at me for a minute. I could tell she was having a hard time trying not to laugh. "Don't worry," she said, finally getting control of herself. "The good thing about hair is that it always grows back."

"Yeah well, that might be the good thing about hair," I snapped, "but what's the good thing about no hair?"

My mother started to giggle. Then she turned and left the room.

"Where are you going?" I yelled. "You've got to help me figure out what to do with all this scalp!"

"I'll be right back," she answered, still snickering. "I'm just going to the kitchen for a minute.

All of a sudden I have this tremendous craving for grapefruit."

"Very funny!" I screamed at her. "Very, very, funny!"

Anyway, right after that I remembered about my baseball cap. I hurried up to my room to find it. I opened up my closet and breathed a sigh of relief. For once I had remembered to put it back on the hook where it belonged. I put it on my head and it slipped down a little bit. Being bald makes your head a lot thinner. I looked in the mirror. Yup. Just like old Steve Garvey! It works every time.

I just wish that putting on a baseball cap could make me hit home runs like Steve Garvey. I guess you could say that hitting a home run is sort of a dream of mine. I don't think it will ever come true, though. My father says that it's pretty hard to hit a home run when all you can do is bunt.

I've always thought "bunt" was a stupid word. The first time I heard it I was only about seven. This kid on my baseball team was on his way up to bat. Before he left the bench, he turned around and said to me, "I think I'm going to bunt."

At first I didn't really know what he was

talking about, but whatever it was, it didn't sound too good. I tried to figure out what he meant, and finally decided that "bunt" was probably another word for "puke."

Oh no, I thought to myself, that kid's sick and no one even knows it! I got off the bench and went running over to the coach and told him that I thought the kid was going to start bunting any minute.

"That's okay, Alex," said the coach, "don't worry about it. I *told* him to bunt."

Now, I was really confused. Why in the world would a coach tell one of his players to throw up? What kind of a trick was this? I hoped he wouldn't tell me to bunt, too.

"Listen, Coach," I said, "I don't think I could bunt even if I wanted to. I feel pretty good and I haven't even eaten dinner yet."

The coach looked at me kind of funny and told me to sit down. I went back to the bench and watched the kid at bat. I wondered when he was going to do it. When the ball came, he took his bat and held it out to the side. I figured he was just trying to get it out of the way so he didn't bunt on it. Since I was next at bat, I thought this was a pretty nice thing to do.

But, instead of getting sick, the kid took the

bat and lightly knocked the ball down the third baseline. He ran as fast as he could and made it to first base in plenty of time.

"Great bunt!" shouted the coach.

I turned to the boy sitting next to me. "I didn't see him bunt. Where is it?"

"Where is what?" he asked.

"You know," I said. "Where is the bunt?"

"Weren't you watching?" he asked. "He just bunted the ball down the third baseline and then ran to first."

Suddenly, I knew what a bunt really was. Brother, did I ever feel like an idiot! Thank goodness no one ever knew what I had been talking about.

Anyway, from that day on, I started working on my bunting. And after four years of practice, I'm probably the best bunter in the entire Little League. I guess that's because no one else bothers working on it very much.

Sometimes Brian helps me practice my bunting at recess. Last week, T.J. saw me and walked over.

"Bunting's for sissies," he said, grinning.

I ignored him.

"Anybody with half a muscle can hit the ball hard," he said.

I still ignored him.

"Hey, Skinnybones, I just thought of something," he said with a smile. "Only runts bunt! Get it? It rhymes!"

That's when I decided to stop ignoring him. Brian pitched me another ball. I held the bat out until the very last minute. Then I turned it sharply so that the ball hit T.J. right on the head.

"Whoops! Sorry there, T.J.," I said. "It seems that all I've been doing lately is accidently hitting you with baseballs. It's a good thing *that* one hit you on the head. Otherwise, you might have gotten hurt."

T.J. walked over, shoved me to the ground, and pounced on top of me. "Well, Mr. Skinnybones, we'll just see how good you bunt on Saturday," he said.

"What happens on Saturday?" I asked. But T.J. didn't understand me. It's hard to speak clearly when your mouth is full of someone's leg.

Then I remembered. Saturday was the day when our Little League teams were scheduled to play each other.

chapter eight

Usually, when I go to the Little League field for a game, I don't know who we're going to play until I get there. I just go to the game, lose, and go home. The way I look at it, losing is losing. Who cares who you lose *to*?

A lot of kids don't feel that way. T.J. is one of them. He's one of those kids who *always* knows exactly which team he's playing, and what their record is. Then, a couple of days before they play, he goes around telling the whole world how the other team is going to get creamed. And the trouble is . . . they know it's true.

The day before we played his team, T.J. went all over the playground shouting out that Franklin's Sporting Goods was going to "mop up the

61

floor" with Fran and Ethel's Cleaning Service.

Fran and Ethel's Cleaning Service—that's the name of my team this year. Neat, huh? When I first found out about it, I thought about quitting. But my father explained to me that Fran and Ethel had paid a lot of money to sponsor our team and that it wouldn't be fair if everyone quit just because it was a stupid name.

So far, I've never had a team name that sounded as neat as Franklin's Sporting Goods. Last year my team was called Preston's Pest Control. Our shirts had pictures of little dead bugs all over them. It was really embarrassing.

Anyway, about five minutes after we got to school on Friday, T.J. raised his hand. When the teacher called on him, he stood up.

"I have an important announcement to make," he said. He looked over at me and smiled. "Tomorrow, at 10:30 A.M., my Little League team is going to be playing Fran and Ethel's Cleaning Service. And, since there are two players in this room that will be playing in that game, I just thought that everyone might enjoy seeing it."

Quickly I raised my hand. I just couldn't let T.J. get away with this. My team hadn't won a game all season, and T.J.'s was in first place. It was going to be humiliating.

The teacher called on me.

"*I* wouldn't," I said.

"You wouldn't what?" asked the teacher with a puzzled look on her face.

"I wouldn't enjoy seeing it," I answered.

"Then don't come," she said simply.

"Thank you, Mrs. Grayson," I said. Then, I sat down with a big fat smile on my face.

T.J. jumped out of his seat. "He *has* to come, Mrs. Grayson! He's playing in the game! If he doesn't show I'll be the only one from our class playing!"

"Okay, then," I said, after the teacher called on me again, "I guess it's all settled. Since there's only *one* kid from our class playing, all the rest of us will stay home and watch cartoons. Tomorrow, *Wolfman Meets the Super Heroes* is on."

By this time, Mrs. Grayson was pretty confused so she dropped the whole thing. But T.J. didn't. As a matter of fact, he talked about it all day long. After school he even stood at the door as the kids were leaving the classroom. As they passed him, he said, "See you at the big game, tomorrow. Don't forget . . . it starts at 10:30!"

"See you tomorrow, chicken," he laughed as I tried to sneak past him.

"Who are you calling chicken?" I demanded.

T.J. grabbed me by the shirt and pulled me

right up to his face. "You. That's who," he said, holding tight.

"I don't mean to be rude, T.J." I said, "but would you mind putting me down? I don't think two people are supposed to be this close unless they're dancing."

T.J. loosened his grip. "Okay, Frankovitch. We'll just see how funny you are tomorrow at the game." Then he smiled and walked away.

Brother, was I ever in for it now! I didn't know what I was going to do. If there's one thing worse than losing, it's losing in front of your whole class.

I've never even played a Little League game in front of a crowd. With a team like mine, you're lucky if even a couple of parents show up. In fact, I hate to admit this, but there are only two people that have shown up at every single game we've played this year . . . Fran and Ethel. They always come to watch us play right after they get off from work. You can tell who they are because they usually stand around wringing out their mops while we warm up.

Anyway, Friday night before the big game, I couldn't sleep at all. I just lay in bed trying to think of a way to get out of playing. I guess I must have thought about it most of the night. But finally, about three o'clock in the morning, I came up with a wonderful idea. I only hoped it would work.

When I went down to breakfast the next morning, I dragged myself into the kitchen on my stomach.

"Good morning, Mom and Dad," I said as I pulled myself over to the breakfast table.

My parents looked down at me on the floor and smiled. "Good morning, Alex," they said together.

"What will you have for breakfast?" asked my mother.

"Cornflakes," I answered, looking up at her.

My mother got up from the table and poured me a bowl of cereal. She stepped over me to get to the refrigerator.

"Juice?" she asked.

I nodded. What was wrong with these people? Didn't they notice that something was wrong with me?

My mother put my breakfast on the floor in front of me. "Better hurry and eat, honey," she said. "You'll have to be dressing for your game soon."

I pushed the cereal and juice out of my way. Then, slowly, I pulled myself over to the table.

When I got there, I pulled my body up into my seat. This whole thing took about ten minutes.

"I think I'd rather eat up here," I said. "Could someone please get me my cornflakes and juice?"

"We're eating right now, Alex," said my dad. "You should have brought your food with you."

Slowly (even slower than before), I leaned down until my hands were on the floor again. The chair flipped over as my body dropped back down. My parents didn't even bother to look up. They were actually ignoring the fact that I couldn't walk!

Finally, I decided to do something really big to get their attention. I pulled myself over to my bowl and started eating my cereal without a spoon. I just put my head in my bowl and started chewing!

After a few minutes of this, my mother walked over to me and dropped a napkin on my head. "You'll probably need this to clean up."

"What kind of parents are you, anyway?" I shouted. "Your poor little son can't walk, and you stand around dropping napkins on his head! Don't you even want to know what happened to me?"

"We already know what happened to you," said my mother calmly.

"You mean that you know about how Ronnie Williams ran over my poor legs with his motorbike last night? And you know about how they stiffened up while I was sleeping? And about how they won't work anymore?"

"No, Alex," my mom said. "We know that your whole class is going to be at your baseball game today. Dad and I will be there, too. Brian's parents called this morning, and we're going over to the game with them."

"Oh," I said quietly.

I finished my cereal on the floor. Then I silently pulled myself back out of the kitchen and down the hallway to my room. Sometimes, when you're caught doing something dumb, you feel too embarrassed to stop doing it right away.

When I got back to my room, I stood up and took my uniform out of the drawer. I put on the shirt. The neck still hung down to my stomach. This was going to be the worst day of my life.

chapter nine

Finally, I decided to head over to the Little League field. As I got close enough to see the baseball diamond, I noticed something very unusual. All around the field, the bleachers were packed with people. And when I say packed, I mean *packed*!

"Whew!" I said feeling a million times better. "Thank goodness! It looks like the high school must be having their graduation here this morning. It must be some sort of mix-up. Now, I won't have to play after all!"

I jumped high into the air. "Yeehaa!" I screeched. As I turned around to head for home, I noticed that the Channel Six News truck was parked alongside the curb.

Wow! I thought to myself. This must really be something *big*. It's even going to be on TV. Then I saw a cameraman get out of the truck.

"Hi," I called to him. "Are you going to put that graduation over there on the news tonight?"

"What graduation?" asked the man. "That's no graduation . . . that's a baseball game."

"A baseball game?" I squeaked.

"Yeah," he continued, "there are two Little League teams playing over there this morning. We're going to film a few minutes of the game to put on the sports news tonight."

"Gee, mister," I said, taking a deep breath. "This must really be an important game to make the weekend sports. What is it . . . the championship or something?"

"Nope," said the cameraman. "It's nothing like that. As a matter of fact, I think that one of these teams I'm going to be filming hasn't won a game all season."

"I'm doomed!" I hollered. Then I flopped down on the curb and put my head in my hands.

"Are you all right?" he asked.

"All right?" I shouted back. "All right? Of course I'm not all right! What kind of man are you anyway, mister? What kind a person would want to embarrass a poor rotten Little League team by showing it on the six o'clock news? What's wrong with you? Do you get your kicks making fun of little kids, or what?"

"Wait a minute there, son," he said. "Calm down. I didn't come to make fun of anyone. It's the other team we're interested in. The one with T. J. Stoner on it. He's the kid we're doing the story on."

"T.J.?" I asked.

"Yep," he explained. "Yesterday we learned that T. J. Stoner has won every single Little League game he's ever played in. That's a record! In fact, if his team wins today, it will be his 125th straight winning game." I just turned and headed toward the field. As I walked away, the cameraman called after me, "Hey, kid, are you going to be playing in that game?"

"Yeah," I yelled. "I'll be the kid fainting in center field."

What else could go wrong? I looked up into the sky. Maybe now was the time to have a little chat with God. After all, that's what he's there for, isn't it?

"Listen, God," I shouted, "if I did something to make you mad, I'm really sorry. And I'll try never to do it again, whatever it is. But right now, I need your help. I'm a good kid, God. Well . . . pretty good. And I really don't think I deserve this. So I'd like to talk to you about making a little deal.

"If you get all those people sitting in the bleachers to go home right now, I'll become a preacher when I grow up. Would you like that, God?"

I looked around to see if anyone was getting up to leave. No luck. In fact, even more people were coming.

"Okay, God," I said, "if you didn't like that deal, how about this one. All you have to do is get rid of the cameraman. If he goes home, I promise to go to church every single Sunday for the rest of my life."

I looked behind me. The cameraman was carrying all his equipment down to the field. He didn't turn around.

"All right, God," I said one last time. "This is my final offer, and it's a good one. All you have to do is whip up one tiny little thunderstorm to get the game canceled and, in return, I will go home this very minute and read the Bible from cover to cover. How's that?"

I looked into the sky. It was the sunniest, clearest day I had seen in months.

"Thanks, God," I said. "Thanks a whole lot. I know I'm not important like Moses or anything, but I really didn't think it would hurt you to do one tiny little miracle."

When I finally got to the field, my team was already there warming up. Every time I looked into the bleachers my knees turned to jelly. I wasn't sure how long they were going to be able to hold me up.

My coach spotted me.

"Frankovitch," my coach shouted when he spotted me, "where in the heck have you been? Get out there in the field and warm up!"

I trotted out to center field.

"Okay, Alex," he hollered, "I'm going to hit you a couple out there. Get ready."

The first ball he hit me was a high pop fly. I was *very* nervous. It seemed like all the people in the bleachers were staring straight at me.

The ball came fast. I didn't even have time to think about it. I just watched it closely, put out my glove, and made a *perfect* catch!

Hmmm, I thought, maybe this isn't going to be so tough, after all. A crowd might be just the thing I need to bring out the best in me.

"Okay, Alex," shouted my coach, again, "here comes another one."

This time it was a hard grounder. As soon as I saw it coming, I ran up to it, bent down, and scooped it up into my glove.

"All right out there, Frankovitch," yelled the coach. "Way to play!"

Boy, was he ever proud of me! The day was turning out a whole lot better than I thought.

chapter ten

The umpire blew his whistle. It was time for the big game to begin.

Our team ran in from the field. On the sideline T.J. was being interviewed for the six o'clock news. I tried to get close enough to listen to what they were saying, but they had just finished. As T.J. walked off, I heard the newsman say, "Good luck out there today, T.J. We're all rooting for you!"

I looked into the bleachers. On the front row sat Fran and Ethel. They were a little bit hard to spot because they didn't have their mops with them. I smiled to myself. Not *everyone's* rooting for you, T.J., I thought.

The umpire's whistle blew again. "Teams take the field!" he shouted.

T.J.'s team ran out to the field. Naturally, T.J. was pitching. He started warming up and, just like in our contest, every ball he threw went zinging over the plate at about sixty miles an hour. I hate to keep saying this, but he really *was* the best Little League pitcher I had ever seen. I sure was glad I didn't have to be up first.

"Batter up!" shouted the ump.

Kevin Murphy was the first batter on our team. As soon as he stepped up to the plate, I could tell he was really nervous. He kept trying to spit, but nothing would come out. Instead, he just kept making this funny sound with his lips. He looked ridiculous.

When T.J. looked at Kevin, he smiled. Then he wound up and threw the ball as hard as he could. Kevin never even saw it go by.

"Steerrriiiikkkee one!" yelled the umpire.

Kevin looked confused. "Did he already throw one?"

T.J. just laughed and went into his windup for his second pitch. This time he threw it a little bit slower. Kevin swung with all his might. But just as the ball got to the plate, it curved.

"Steerrriiiikkkee two!" screamed the umpire

again. Poor Kevin hadn't even come close. I *really* felt sorry for him. Whenever you swing as hard as you can and miss it, you always feel like an idiot. Kevin tried acting tough but, when he went to spit again, he just made that same stupid sound with his lips.

Quickly, he took his bat back and got ready for the next pitch. But unfortunately, the third ball that T.J. threw was even better than the first two. Kevin just watched it go streaking by.

"Strike three! Batter's out!" yelled the ump.

Everyone in the stands began to cheer loudly for T.J. Kevin sat down on the bench and began to cry. He couldn't seem to stop. After a while, his mother had to be called out of the bleachers to get him calmed down. At first the whole team was pretty embarrassed about it. But as it turned out, Kevin was the best batter of the inning. He was the only one who swung.

The second batter, Willy Jenson, didn't even *try* to swing. And by the time the third batter got up, he was so nervous, he didn't even bother to put the bat up to his shoulder. He just stood there, let three pitches go by, and sat down.

Our team was out in the field before we knew it. Everyone was looking pretty sad. What we really needed was a pep talk to get the old team spirit going. So I called all the guys into a huddle.

76

"Okay, you guys," I said, trying to act real peppy. "All we need to do is hold them. What do you say? Let's get them out one-two-three! Three up. Three down!"

The first baseman looked at me and laughed right out loud. "Frankovitch, you jerk," he said, "who do you think you're kidding? Our team hasn't made three outs in a row all year!"

"Yeah, Alex," said the catcher. "We're lucky if we make three outs the whole game. So why don't you just shut up and get out to center field where you belong?"

So much for the old team spirit. But I didn't care what they said. I was going to cheer our team on, whether they wanted me to or not.

Frankie Rogers was going to be our starting pitcher. As I walked out to center field, I watched him warm up. He threw twice and said he was ready. Frankie doesn't like to warm up for too long. He only throws a couple of good balls a game, and he doesn't want to risk throwing them in practice.

I started cheering. "Okay, Frankie, pitch it in there, babe. Right over the plate, Frankie! You can do it!"

Frankie threw the first ball. It hit the dirt about ten feet in front of the plate.

"Ball one!" shouted the umpire.

"That's okay, Frankie, don't worry. You can do it, babe!" I yelled.

All of a sudden Frankie asked the umpire for time-out. Then he turned and walked out toward center field. At first I figured he was probably coming out to thank me for cheering. But when he got close enough, I could see he wasn't smiling. I walked up to meet him.

"Will you please shut up, Alex?" he screamed. "You're really getting on my nerves! How in the world am I supposed to concentrate with all that shouting going on out here?"

"That's not shouting, Frankie, that's cheering!" I told him. "I'm just trying to encourage you a little bit."

"Yeah well, if you ask me, you're acting like a jerk. So how about just shutting up?" Frankie said, stomping back to the pitcher's mound.

As he got ready to throw his next pitch, I yelled, "Okay, Frankie, throw any dumb kind of pitch you want. See if *I* care!"

The ball zoomed toward the plate but, unfortunately, it was just a little bit low. It hit the batter on the foot and he took his base. The next batter hurried up to the plate. Once again, Frankie got ready. This time, he hit the kid at bat in the arm.

If you ask me, he was embarrassing the whole

team. It was bad enough that he couldn't pitch. But to make matters worse, he didn't even throw the ball hard enough to hurt anyone.

I looked over to the sidelines. The news camera was rolling. "Oh no!" I said to myself. I put both my hands over my face so that no one would recognize me on the six o'clock news.

While I was standing there with my face covered up, I heard a big loud crack. I looked up. Some kid had hit the ball and was running to first base.

Everyone began to holler and scream. Then, all the guys on my team turned to look at me. At first I wasn't sure why, so I just sort of smiled. But suddenly I realized that they were watching to see if I was going to catch the ball which was probably headed my way. I panicked. I didn't even know where the ball was! I looked up into the sky to try and find it, but I couldn't see it anywhere! The worst feeling in the world is knowing that any minute a hard ball is going to smack you right in the head, and you don't know where it's coming from.

I had to try to protect myself. Quickly I took my glove off my hand and put it on my head. It was just in time! I felt something hit my glove with a big thud! I felt it roll off the top of my head and land on the ground next to me.

My team started going crazy. "Oh no! He dropped it! He dropped the stupid ball!" they screamed.

"I did not!" I screamed back at them. "How can a person drop something when he didn't even catch it in the first place? Just because something lands on your head does not mean that you caught it!"

"It does too!" shouted the third baseman. "You caught it on your head, and then dropped it!"

"If a bird poops on your head, you don't say that you've caught it, do you, you jerk?" I yelled back.

I was so busy arguing that I forgot all about the ball. By the time I remembered, it was too late. Three runs had already scored.

The coach was waving at me from the sidelines. Just to be polite, I waved back.

"He's not waving, Frankovitch, you jerk," shouted the left fielder. "He's shaking his fists!"

I looked closer. Yup. Those were fists, all right. He was even madder than I thought.

It took a few minutes for things to settle back down. Frankie got ready to face his fourth batter. I looked to see who was up. My heart began to pound.

Slowly T.J. walked up to the plate and took a few practice swings. Then he knocked the dirt off his shoes and pointed to me in center field. My stomach started doing flips. Oh no, I thought to myself. He's going to slam it right to me! Nervously, I backed up. If I made another mistake out there, I was doomed.

Frankie pitched the ball. T.J. pulled the bat back and hit it with all his might. It was a hard grounder, and just as I thought, headed my way!

I watched it as it bounced over second base and started into center field. If only I could remember what the coach had told me about catching hard grounders! If only I could get T. J. Stoner out!

I tried to do everything just like in the big leagues. First, I ran up to meet the ball. Then, I stooped down directly in front of it. I even kept my eye on it. It's almost here! I thought. I've got it! I've got it!

But just as it was about to roll into my glove, it hit a small dirt mound and took a crazy bounce to the right.

"Oh no!" I screamed. I made a diving leap trying to stop it, but it was no use. The ball sped away and kept right on rolling all the way to the back fence.

The crowd went wild. I looked at T.J. as he

was running the bases. He saw me and tipped his cap. What a big shot! He really made me sick!

My coach was screaming for me to get the ball. But I was just too mad. "He hit it!" I hollered, pointing at T.J. "Let *him* go get it!"

Finally, the left fielder went out to retrieve the ball. My coach's face got so red, I could see it from center field. For a minute there, I actually thought he might blow up. Boy, was I in trouble now. I figured it might be a good time to have another little chat with God.

"God, please, whatever you do, don't let our team get up to bat again until my coach settles down. If I have to go over there now, he's going to kill me, God, I know he will. And if you think I'm a problem down here, just imagine what it would be like to have me running around heaven with you. You'd never have a minute's peace, God. Think about it."

Right after I finished talking to God, I watched as Frankie threw nine straight strikes in a row!

"I've done something to upset you, haven't I, God?" I said, looking up to the sky. Then I thought a minute. "If you're still mad about me wearing a gorilla costume in the Christmas play, it wasn't my fault. I told my teacher at least fifty times that I did *not* want to be one of those sheep in the manger."

All the kids on my team were passing me as they headed for the bench. I saw the coach waiting for me on the sideline. He had a very strange grin on his face and kept pounding his fist into his hand. As I walked by, he grabbed my arm and handed me a bat.

I forced a smile. "Someday we'll look back on this and laugh," I said quietly.

"Yeah, Frankovitch," he growled, his teeth clenched together. "You and I are going to do a whole lot of laughing right after the game. But right now you're up. So get your tail over there." Then he gave me a little shove toward home plate.

I dropped my glove on the ground and looked around as I headed toward the batter's box. Sitting in the stands, Fran and Ethel were clapping. Standing on the sideline, the camera-man was filming. And waiting on the mound in front of me, T. J. Stoner was grinning.

This was easily the worst moment of my life. There was no escape. No joke would save me now.

"Get going, Alex!" screamed my coach from behind me.

I gulped and stepped up to the plate. T.J.

began to laugh. Then he turned around and hollered to the rest of his team.

"Easy out! Easy out!" He screamed loud enough for the whole world to hear.

All the guys in the infield took four giant steps in. That didn't do much for my confidence.

"Get ready for a bunt!" yelled T.J.

Oh wonderful! I thought to myself. Now everyone knows exactly what I'm going to do. But I didn't really have a choice. It was either bunt or not hit it at all.

T.J. threw his first pitch. Whoosh! I couldn't believe how fast it came streaking over the plate!

"Steerrriiiikkkee one!" shouted the umpire.

Why do umpires always have to yell "strike" so loud? Whenever it's a ball they practically whisper. But as soon as they see a strike, they act like everyone's deaf or something.

I made up my mind that I wasn't going to just stand there like an idiot and let another ball go by. If I was going to strike out, I was going to do it swinging.

T.J. wound up and threw again. Quickly, I stuck out my bat. As the ball whizzed over the plate, it hit the bat on the corner and began rolling toward first base.

I couldn't believe it. I started running as fast

as I could. If only I could get on base. I'd be a hero! And no one can be mad at a hero. Not even my coach.

The first baseman ran toward me to pick up the ball. Meanwhile, T.J. ran over to cover first.

Everyone was going crazy. My coach was jumping up and down as I passed him running to first. He didn't even look mad anymore. I just had to make it!

The first baseman picked up the ball and got ready to make the throw. I was almost there. Just three more steps to go.

He threw. T.J. got ready for the catch. I had to do something!

"BOOGA BOOGA!" I screamed suddenly, flinging my arms all around. "BOOGA BOOGA!"

T.J. looked surprised. And for just a split second he took his eye off the ball. It shot past him and rolled into the outfield. I WAS SAFE!

As the outfielders scrambled for the ball, I took a chance and headed for second.

"Legs, don't fail me now!" I yelled as I hit full speed. I didn't look back until I was safe at second.

The crowd in the stands went wild.

"I did it! I did it!" I screamed. "A double! I got a double!"

The second baseman told me to shut up. But I ignored him. No one could ruin this moment for me, not the second baseman, not T. J. Stoner, not anyone!

But something didn't look quite right. From second base, I watched as T.J.'s coach ran onto the field and began arguing with the umpire. And before I knew it, my coach was out there, too.

I couldn't figure out what the problem could be. The whole thing was so simple. T.J. had missed the ball and I got a double. A double! Wow! I still couldn't believe it. I started jumping up and down all over again.

Out in the field, my coach had started jumping up and down right along with me. But for some reason he didn't look very happy. All of a sudden, I saw the umpire begin to walk out toward second base.

Don't panic, Alex, I thought. Maybe he's not really coming to second base at all. Maybe during all that excitement, someone threw toilet paper streamers onto the outfield and the umpire's walking out there to clean them up. But in a few seconds, the umpire was standing next to me at second base.

He leaned right down in my face and screamed, "You're out!"

86

"Out?" I asked, puzzled. "How could I be out? I bunted!"

"You interfered with the play at first base," he said.

"I did not!" I argued. "I didn't even touch T.J.!"

"You jumped up and down and shouted 'booga booga,'" said the umpire.

My coach ran up behind the umpire and held out his rule book. "Show me where it says you can't say 'booga booga!'" he demanded. "Tell me, huh? What page is the 'no bogga booga' rule on?"

I don't know why, but suddenly this whole conversation seemed pretty funny. I looked up at the umpire and smiled. "Booga booga," I said quietly.

"Get off the field, you smart aleck," he ordered.

I nodded my head. "Booga," I said again softly.

Then, slowly I began trotting off the field toward the bench. As I was running, I could see T.J. out of the corner of my eye. He had started to laugh. Only I knew he wasn't laughing *with* me. He was laughing *at* me.

I just couldn't let him get away with it. Suddenly, I got an idea. If T.J. wanted to laugh, I might as well give him something to laugh about.

87

Quickly, I changed my direction and began running right toward him. When he looked up and saw me coming, he stopped laughing. I guess he wasn't quite sure what kind of crazy thing I was going to do next.

When I got to the pitcher's mound, I jumped up and down a couple of times, then quickly lifted up his arm and started tickling him. "Booga booga," I said, poking at his ribs.

For the first time in his life, T.J. looked embarrassed. It was great while it lasted, but unfortunately, it didn't last too long. After a couple of seconds he began to look extremely angry. That's when I decided to split.

I ran off the field as fast as I could, and then out the gate. I didn't slow down until I was safely in my own room. Locking the door behind me, I had a feeling that I wouldn't want to come out for a long, long, time.

chapter eleven

I stayed in my room for about an hour before I heard my parents come home from the game. I had pushed my dresser over in front of the door so that no one could get in. I wasn't sure exactly what my father was going to do when he got home, but I had a pretty good idea.

I figured he would probably knock on my door and tell me he wanted to talk to me. When I let him in, he would sit down on the bed and just stare at me for a while. Then he would start one of those big "talks" that parents love to have with their children, and that children hate to have with their parents.

He would start off by telling me that running

away from a problem never solves anything. Then he would say that he hoped I wouldn't keep trying to make a big joke out of everything I'm not good at. And he would end up by telling me that "no matter what you try to do in life, you must always try to do the best you can." Then he would ask me if I understood what he was trying to tell me.

"Yes," I would answer, "I think that you're trying to tell me never to do anything stupid to embarrass the family again."

Then my father would stare at me for a minute, shake his head, and start out of my room. On his way out he would probably mutter something like, "I might as well be talking to a brick wall."

All of a sudden I heard the back door open and close. My heart started to pound. I listened to the sound of Dad's footsteps coming down the hall.

Here it comes, I thought to myself. Next he's going to knock on my door and tell me that he wants to have a little talk.

Knock, knock, knock. . . .

"Who is it?" I asked, as if I didn't know.

"It's Dad."

"Dad who?"

"Come on, Alex," said my father. "Open the door. I want to talk to you a minute."

"I already know what you want, Dad," I replied. "You want to talk to me about what happened today. And you probably even think that by talking it out, you can make me feel better. But you might as well save your breath, Dad. It's no use. The way I feel, no one in the whole world could make me feel better. So if you don't mind, I've decided to become a hermit and live right here in my room for the rest of my life. If you or Mom would just shove a bologna sandwich under the door every once in a while, I'd really appreciate it.

"And one more thing, Dad," I added. "Don't try and force your way in here to try and save me. I shoved my dresser up against the door, and I wouldn't want you to hurt yourself."

I figured that by this time, my father was really feeling sorry for me.

"Well, Dad," I said, "it's been real nice having you for a father. I'll see you when I'm all grown-up."

I heard my father leave my door and walk back down the hall toward the kitchen. I knew he was probably going to tell my mother what had happened. Then the two of them would sit down together and try to figure out a way to get me to come out.

A few minutes later, I heard a noise at my door. Aha! I thought to myself. There they are now! They're probably going to stand there and beg me to come out!

But something behind the dresser was making a funny sound. When I looked to see what it was, I saw a bologna sandwich in a plastic bag, being squeezed underneath the space at the bottom of my door.

"Very funny, Dad!" I yelled. "Very, very funny!"

I grabbed the flattened sandwich and threw it in my trash can. Parents! Just when you think you've got them all figured out, they go and pull a dumb trick like that.

The next day was Sunday. And, except for a few minutes while my parents were at church, I didn't come out of my room all day long.

The thing that bothered me most about staying in there all day was that my parents didn't seem to care at all. In fact, every once in a while, I could even hear them laughing. What kind of people think it's funny for a kid to spend the rest of his life shut away in a tiny bedroom?

The other thing that bothered me was how boring it was. Most of the time I just lay on my bed. There were probably better things to be doing, but just in case someone looked through the window to see me, I didn't want it to seem like I was having a good time.

By dinner time, I was really wanting to come out. I could hear my mother starting to make dinner in the kitchen. Boy, was I ever hungry! I had hardly eaten a thing all day.

While my parents were at church I had snuck a few snacks and a couple of apples, but it wasn't nearly enough to keep a growing boy going. Besides, all I had left were two pretzels and one broken graham cracker. I tried putting the pretzels between the graham cracker pieces to make a sandwich, but it looked terrible.

Being hungry wasn't my biggest problem, though. I had to go to the bathroom worse than I've ever had to go in my whole entire life. I waited as long as I could, but finally, I just couldn't stand it one more minute. I pushed the dresser away from the door and ran to the bathroom. I know my parents must have heard me, but no one even bothered to walk down the hall to see how I was. On the way back to my room, I heard them sitting down to dinner. I could smell the delicious aroma all the way down the hall.

I began to wonder how long a person could go without food before he passed out and died. The thought made me very nervous. My stomach started to growl loudly. I decided that maybe if I just got a little peek at some real food, it might make me feel better.

Quietly, I tiptoed down the hall toward the kitchen. Just one little peek . . . that's all I wanted. I stopped at the kitchen door and got down on my hands and knees. Slowly, I peeked around the corner.

Fried chicken and corn on the cob. I just couldn't stand it! My mouth had begun to water so much that I almost started drooling down the front of my shirt.

My parents were staring at me. Neither one of them said anything. They kept right on eating!

"Listen, Mom and Dad," I said, "you might as well forget trying to pretend I'm not here. I know you can see me."

My father looked up. "You're the one who doesn't want anyone to bother you, Alex," he said. "It wasn't our idea."

"Well, maybe I've changed my mind," I said, staring at all the corn on the cob, piled high in a bowl in the middle of the table. Butter was melting down the sides. I sat down in my chair.

"Chicken?" asked my father.

"I am not!" I shouted angrily. "Just because I ran off the Little League field doesn't mean I'm a chicken!"

My father gave me a real disgusted look and then just shook his head. "Chicken?" he said to my mother as he picked up the plate and handed it to her.

"Yes, please," said my mother as she took a big piece of fried chicken off the plate.

My father turned to me and said, "Shall we try it again, Alex? Chicken?" Then he passed me the plate.

I managed to mumble "thank you" but that was the last word I said the entire meal.

My parents tried to talk to me about what happened at the game, but I just couldn't do it. It's bad enough when you act like an idiot, but it's even worse when you have to talk about it.

After dinner, I went back to my room and fed the rest of the graham cracker and the pretzels to my fish. Then I got my pajamas on and went straight to bed. I knew that my parents would make me go to school the next day, and I was going to need a lot of energy to face the kids in my class.

chapter twelve

One of the things I really hate about my mother is that she always seems to know when I'm lying. Don't ask me how she does it. I've tried to figure it out, but so far I've had no luck at all.

On Monday morning, when she came into my room to get me out of bed, I started moaning and groaning and holding my sides.

"Ohhhh . . ." I wailed, "my stomach, my stomach."

My mother rolled up my window shade. "What a nice sunny day out there," she said cheerfully.

"Ohhhh!" I cried loudly, trying to get her attention. "I'm not kidding, Mom. It really hurts! I think I'm dying."

"Okay, Alex," she said standing at the end of my bed with her arms crossed. "If you want me to play this little game with you . . . fine. Now I guess I'm supposed to ask you what's wrong with your stomach."

"Aaggg," I said, doubling over in pain. "It must have been something I ate. Maybe there was something wrong with the chicken I had last night for dinner."

My mother casually strolled over to my dresser and looked down into my fish bowl. "Did your fish have chicken for dinner, too?" she asked.

"Don't try to make me laugh, Mom," I said. "It hurts too much."

"I'm not trying to make you laugh, Alex," said my mother. "Your fish is dead."

"Oh no!" I shouted. I jumped out of bed and ran over to the goldfish bowl. "He's not dead! He can't be!"

"Maybe he's just trying to learn how to float on his back," said my mother with a little laugh.

"How can you make a joke about this?" I hollered.

"Oh, for heaven's sake, Alex," she answered, "you've only had that fish for four days. Your fish never last more than a week. How much can a four-day-old fish mean to you? I would think that by this time, you'd be used to them dying. So far this month, you've already overfed five of them."

"It doesn't matter. I still don't think that you should make fun of someone's pet dying," I insisted.

I got my little fish net and scooped up my dead fish. Then I ran him into the bathroom and flushed him down the toilet. When I got back to my room, my mother was standing there with a smile on her face.

"I see that your stomach is better," she said. "You haven't moaned or groaned for several minutes."

"Ohhhh," I said quickly, grabbing my sides and bending over.

"Forget it, Alex. It won't work. Get dressed. You're going to school," she said, leaving the room.

"I blew it!" I said to myself. I almost had her believing me and I blew it. If it wasn't for that stupid fish, I wouldn't have had to go to school. Boy, you try to do your pet a favor by giving him a special dessert, and this is how he thanks you. He dies. What a pal.

On the way to school, I tried to plan what I would say to the kids when I got there. I knew that everyone was going to be making fun of the way that I had acted at the game. And what made it even worse was that I also knew that T. J. Stoner was going to be the big fat hero.

As I got near the playground, I could already see about a million kids gathered around T.J. They were asking him for his autograph! All those jerky kids were actually asking T. J. Stoner for his autograph!

I rushed by in a hurry to get to my classroom. Luckily, no one saw me. I figured that if I could just get to my desk before class started, no one would have a chance to make fun of me.

I was wrong. When I walked into the classroom, my teacher looked up and started to giggle. "Ooga ooga," she said.

I frowned. "It wasn't 'ooga, ooga,' Mrs. Grayson," I said disgustedly. " 'Ooga ooga' is the sound an old-fashioned car makes. What I *said* was, 'booga booga.' "

"Oh," she said quietly, looking a little embarrassed. "It was hard to hear you from the stands."

"Mrs. Grayson, I was wondering if I could sit in the back of the room today?" I asked. "I'm feeling a little sick and I might need to run to the bathroom from time to time."

Before Mrs. Grayson had a chance to answer me, the bell rang and everyone started rushing in to take their seats.

"Hey, look who's here," shouted T.J. "It's Booga Booga Frankovitch!" The whole class started laughing at once.

"Would you like to go to the nurse?" Mrs. Grayson shouted over the laughter.

"No thanks," I yelled even louder. "If I feel like I'm going to toss my cookies, I'll just aim for T.J. He's a pretty good catch."

"What a threat!" laughed T.J. "If you toss your cookies like you toss a baseball, you'll miss me by a mile."

"That's enough," said Mrs. Grayson, motioning for both of us to sit down.

I was glad she stepped in. For the first time in my life, I didn't have anything else to say.

T.J. raised his hand. "Mrs. Grayson," he said after he was called on, "would it be all right if I finished signing a couple of autographs for some of the kids in the room? I didn't have a chance to finish before class."

Mrs. Grayson smiled. "Sure, T.J.," she answered. "I think we can spare a few minutes to let the National Little League Champion sign a few autographs."

Everyone started clapping. I couldn't believe it! You might have thought he was Tom Seaver or something!

"Boys and girls," said Mrs. Grayson, "I really think that we're very fortunate to have T.J. in our room this year. In case any of you missed it on the news Saturday night, T. J. Stoner is going to be in the *Guinness Book of World Records*! He now holds the record for the most games ever won in a row in the history of Little League baseball!"

More applause.

I couldn't stand it one more minute. Quickly I got out my notebook and scribbled a message to Brian. It read:

"Say something nice about me and I'll give you a dollar after school."

Brian's hand shot up in the air like a bullet. Brian loves money more than any kid I know.

"Yes, Brian?" said Mrs. Grayson.

"Mrs. Grayson," he began, "I think we're also fortunate to have Alex Frankovitch in our class this year. If you ask me, it takes a very special person to stand in front of a crowd and make a big buffoon out of himself like Alex did."

This time even Mrs. Grayson couldn't keep from laughing. When I become popular, I think Brian will be the first friend I'll dump.

The rest of the day I tried to stay as quiet as I could. I wanted to make it as easy as possible for people to ignore me. But it didn't work. All day long, whenever anyone walked by my desk, they would lean over and whisper 'booga booga' in my ear as they passed. Then they'd walk away and laugh as if they were the first one to think of it.

By one o'clock I just couldn't take it one more second. That's when Harold Marshall raised his hand and asked if he could sharpen his pencil. Harold's a troublemaker, so he has to ask permission to do anything.

Mrs. Grayson nodded her head and Harold started up my row to the pencil sharpener. I was positive that when he passed my desk he would try to get in a couple of quick boogas. So as he got closer to my seat, I got ready for him.

Just as Harold leaned over to whisper in my ear, I quickly turned my face in his direction, making it look as if he had just leaned over and kissed me.

I jumped up. "Yuck! Did you see that?" I yelled wiping off my face. "Harold Marshall just kissed me on the cheek! How revolting!"

Harold started turning red. "I did not!" he sputtered.

"Then how did my cheek get so wet?" I asked

pointing to my face. "Mrs. Grayson, can I go to the bathroom and wash it off? I think I'm allergic to slobber."

Mrs. Grayson motioned me out the door and ordered Harold to sit down. As I left the room, I saw several kids covering their faces as Harold passed by.

Unfortunately, making a fool out of Harold didn't really change anything. As soon as I got back from the bathroom, the booga boogas started all over again.

I looked at the clock. Only forty-five minutes to go. I just didn't know if I could make it that long. I began feeling sorry for myself. It seemed like nothing I had ever done had turned out right. Even when I did something well, like bunting for instance, it turned out wrong.

"Let's face it Alex," I finally said to myself, "the only thing that you've ever really succeeded at is being short. You're a nothing. A big fat nothing!"

I leaned my head down and rested it on my desk. I felt my eyes starting to get wet. Oh terrific! I thought. Now big fat nothing Alex Frankovitch is going to cry in front of the whole class.

Suddenly, I heard my name being called. I

didn't look up. "*Alex Frankovitch?*" said the voice again. But it wasn't my teacher. Quickly I wiped a tear out of my eye and looked up. The voice was coming from the loudspeaker on the wall.

It was our principal, Mr. Vernon. "*Mrs. Grayson, is Alex Frankovitch there?*" he asked.

"Yes he is, Mr. Vernon," she answered. "Would you like me to send him down to your office?"

"*No,*" said Mr. Vernon. "*I have an announcement to make about him and I just wanted to be sure that he was there.*"

My heart started beating wildly. T.J. pointed at me and started to laugh. We both figured we knew what was coming. Mr. Vernon was going to make a couple more booga-booga jokes so the whole school could have a good laugh.

Mr. Vernon clicked on the loudspeaker so that all the other classrooms could hear him.

"*Attention, boys and girls, may I have your attention, please?*

"*First of all, I'd like to congratulate T. J. Stoner on his brilliant Little League performance! The entire school is very, very proud of him. I think that we should all give him a big round of applause!*"

Then he stopped a minute so that all the classrooms could clap.

"*By the way*," he continued, "*I have already spoken to T.J. today, and he has agreed to stay after school in case any of you would like to stop by and get his autograph. We'll have a table set up for him in the Multipurpose Room.*"

T.J. just sat there and grinned like a big shot. I wished I had my dead fish back. I would have put it down his shirt.

"*Now then,*" Mr. Vernon's voice came back through the loudspeaker. "*There's someone else in Mrs. Grayson's sixth-grade room that I'd also like to congratulate.*"

Here it comes, I thought to myself. He's going to congratulate me for being the biggest buffoon in the school.

"*It seems that Alex Frankovitch has also made quite a name for himself.*"

I could feel everyone's eyes staring at my back. A few kids were already giggling. Tears started to fill my eyes again, but I forced them back into my head.

"*I have just received news from his mother, that today Alex Frankovitch got a letter in the mail announcing that he is the winner of the National Kitty Fritters Television Contest! And according to the letter, as his prize, Alex will get to appear in a national television commercial!*

"Congratulations, Alex! We're all very excited about having one of our students become a big TV star!"

The whole class was completely silent. No one could believe what Mr. Vernon had said. Especially me! I only wrote that letter as a joke!

After a few seconds I guess the shock wore off, and everyone started clapping. Mrs. Grayson told me to stand up and take a bow, but my legs were so weak I couldn't get out of my chair. So I just turned around and waved instead.

Just then, my mother appeared in the doorway. Mrs. Grayson went to greet her and called me to the front of the room.

"How was that for a big surprise?" asked my mother when she saw me. "I was going to tell you in person, but I happened to see Mr. Vernon on the way down the hall, and we decided it might be more fun to surprise you with it over the loudspeaker. Were you surprised?"

I nodded. Up until this time, I had been unable to say anything. It's hard to form words when your mouth is hanging wide open.

"When do you get to do the commercial?" asked Mrs. Grayson.

"I'm not sure," I said finally, trying to think back to the instructions on the contest sheet. "I just entered that contest as a joke," I admitted. "I didn't really pay much attention to the prize."

My mother waved a piece of paper in front of my face. "It says here that the commercial will be made in New York sometime within the next six months!" she said proudly. "They also said that your contest entry was the funniest, most original essay that they had ever received. And they can't wait to meet you!"

Mrs. Grayson put her hand on my shoulder. "This might just be your start in show business!" she said. Then she and my mother both laughed.

Well I hate to tell them, but they just might be right. Once those Kitty Fritters people get a hold of me, they'll probably never want to let me go. I smiled at the thought of it.

After a few more minutes, my mother left the classroom and went home. Since the day was almost over, Mrs. Grayson told us to put all our work away.

"I just got a great idea," she said. "Why don't we have our two class celebrities come up here and answer questions like they do on TV?"

Since I was already in the front of the room, I casually got up from my seat and sat down on the front edge of Mrs. Grayson's desk. T.J. was a little slower getting there. But finally he shuffled up and sat down next to me. I could tell he really hated sharing his big day with me.

"Okay," said Mrs. Grayson. "Who has questions?"

Harold Marshall's hand was up like a bullet.

"Yes, Harold?" said T.J. quickly.

Harold stood up. "I have a question for Alex," he said, laughing. T.J. smiled. I was sure he already knew what Harold was going to ask. They had probably set it up before T.J. came to the front of the room.

"What exactly is a booga booga?" he asked, cracking up.

I knew it! I knew he was going to say something like that!

I thought a minute before I answered. "It's hard to explain," I said after a minute. "A booga booga is sort of a big wad of green slimy . . . wait a minute! What a coincidence! If everyone will turn around quickly, there's a booga booga sitting in Harold's hair right now!"

Everybody started laughing all at once. Everybody except Harold, that is. Mrs. Grayson didn't seem to mind. I guess she knew that Harold deserved it.

After that, Harold didn't give me any more trouble and T.J. and I started answering questions. Melissa Phillips asked each of us who our most famous relative was. T.J. said it was his brother, Matt Stoner. I said it was my grandmother, Steve Garvey.

Most of the questions were about the *Guinness Book of World Records*. But I didn't really mind. It felt good just sitting up there.

I looked over at T.J. as he answered a question from Adam Brooks. T.J. was a creep all right. But maybe it wasn't all his fault. I had a feeling that being a big shot can make a creep out of anyone if they're not careful. Even a wonderful guy like me. Maybe I better not dump Brian after all, I thought to myself. It might be bad for my image.

"That's all we have time for today," said Mrs. Grayson. "If we have any free time tomorrow, we can continue."

I went to my desk and picked up my homework books. After the bell rang, I filed out of the room with everyone else. As I passed by Mrs. Grayson, she patted me on the back. Maybe after all these years I'd finally done it. Maybe I'd finally found a teacher who liked my sense of humor.

Outside the building, Brian was waiting for me. When he saw me coming, he smiled. I didn't.

"Oh no you don't," I said. "Just because I'm famous and popular doesn't mean you can come crawling back to me. I'm not forgetting how you called me a buffoon."

Brian got a puzzled look on his face. "What are you talking about, Alex?" he asked. "Who's crawling back? I'm just waiting to collect the buck you promised me for saying something nice."

"You call buffoon, nice?"

"I didn't call you a buffoon, Alex," he corrected. "If I had called you a buffoon I would have only charged you fifty cents. I called you a *big* buffoon. That's a dollar. You get twice the buffoon for your money."

I couldn't keep myself from laughing. It's hard to stay mad at Brian. We started walking home together. As we walked, a couple of kids congratulated me on the TV commercial. No one asked for an autograph, but I figure that will probably come later.

On the way home, Brian and I talked a lot about my future as a comedian. We decided that as long as I've already gotten my first break into show business, I might as well go on to become disgustingly rich. I told Brian that I would think about letting him write some of my material. "Material" is the word comedians use when they talk about their jokes.

I still can't get over it. Me, skinny little Alex Frankovitch, a star. Hmm. I wonder if the Kitty Fritters people will want me to read my winning essay on the commercial. No, they'll probably just want to use my cute little face smiling at a cat food bag or something. I just hope they don't want me to do anything dumb. Sometimes these commercials can get pretty crazy.

One time I saw a cereal commercial where they made this little kid dress up like a raisin and dance around a big bowl of oatmeal. Boy, the thought of doing something like that really gives me the creeps. Hmm. Maybe it's time for another little chat.

"Hello, God? It's Alex Frankovitch again. Listen, I have another little favor I'd like to ask. As you probably know I'm going to be on a TV commercial soon. And well, I'd *really* appreciate it if I didn't have to dress up like a Kitty Fritter and dance around a cat dish. I mean, I don't mind making a fool of myself once in a while, God. But I do have my pride.

"Are you listening, God? If you are, please just do me this one little favor, and I promise to stop singing 'doo-da' at the end of the hymns in church, and start singing "Amen" like everyone else. How's that? Is it a deal, God? If it is, show me by making the wind start blowing.

111

"Aha! I saw it. I saw a little leaf move on that tree over there. Thanks a lot, God! I *knew* I could count on you.

"And remember, if you ever need a favor, you can count on me, too. Just look me up in New York or Hollywood.

"I'll be in the *Yellow Pages* under 'Star.' "

BARBARA PARK is one of the most popular authors writing for young readers today. Her novels include *Almost Starring Skinnybones, The Kid in the Red Jacket, Buddies, Beanpole, Skinnybones, Operation: Dump the Chump,* and *Don't Make Me Smile.*

Ms. Park holds a B.S. in education from the University of Alabama and lives in Phoenix, Arizona, with her husband and two sons.